THE LOVE NEXT DOOR

TEXAS MAIL ORDER BRIDES

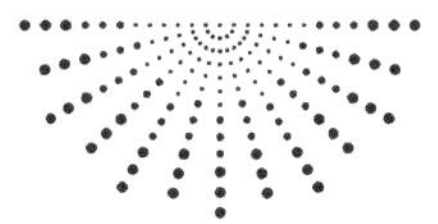

INDIANA WAKE

BELLE FIFFER

SWEETBOOKHUB.COM

CHAPTER ONE

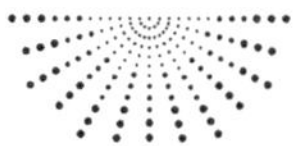

"There you go, little man." Sean Price picked up the baby and bounced him in his arms as he carried the boy to his mother. "All done. That wasn't so bad, was it?"

Oliver cooed in his arms, his wet hands trying to grab onto the stethoscope around Sean's neck.

Cecily chuckled and plucked her son out of the doctor's arms. "Honestly, Oliver, you need to stop doing that. Everything's going to be covered in sticky saliva."

"That's nothing compared to what I'm normally covered in." Sean chuckled. He tickled Oliver's cheek, which made the boy giggle. "He's come through his check-up with flying colors, he's in good health. He's growing at the pace that he should be, and he is very happy in himself. You've done really well with him, Cecily."

Cecily knew she was blushing. She glanced away and focused on bouncing Oliver on her knee.

"I wouldn't say that. I'm getting by."

"And you're doing yourself a disservice by not thinking you're doing well."

Cecily didn't think she was doing too badly. Oliver was happy and healthy, and he wasn't often getting up in the night. For the most part, he slept well, and so did Cecily. But there was a part of her that made her feel awful that she wasn't up at night all the time like other mothers. It was a stupid thing to be worried about, she knew, but there were a lot of people talking.

She hadn't planned on becoming a widow raising a child on her own. But things happened, and her husband died suddenly. So close to her giving birth, Cecily had panicked about how she was going to cope. Sure, she had family, and there were her in-laws as well, but she didn't like imposing on anyone. Besides, her family was overbearing and would have taken Oliver off her to raise him their way; she wouldn't have had a say in his upbringing at all.

So, when she had given birth, Cecily had been so hysterical about raising a child on her own that she had left Oliver at the schoolhouse to be raised by someone else. She was incredibly lucky that she was found when a search was started for the mother; otherwise, she would have died in her bed due to blood loss and she wouldn't have this little mite. It felt awful now, looking back and realizing she was afraid of failing as a mother after she lost the man she loved.

It had taken some time before she was fully recovered, and a little more to properly bond with Oliver, but Cecily had persevered. So many people supported her during that time. Sean was one, Molly and Emma also helped out, and her neighbor, Lewis had even given her a job helping out at his printing shop. Between him and his brother, Christian, they made sure she had an income and even let her bring Oliver along. There didn't seem to be any issues between them.

Cecily would be forever grateful to everyone who supported her. It was what she needed after suffering alone. Lewis, especially, was a godsend.

"How are things going with Lewis being your boss?" Sean asked as he went to his desk. "I know he's got a reputation of working everyone really hard, so I hope he's not doing the same with you."

"He's absolutely fine. He allows me to focus on Oliver when I need to." Cecily smiled as she thought of her husband's friend. "He even looks after Oliver, if needed."

"I didn't think he was fond of children. He's said that he wouldn't have them himself."

"I thought that myself. So, you can imagine my surprise when he said he wanted to help me out. He's even changed diapers even though he hates that sort of mess."

Sean arched an eyebrow. "He changed diapers? What have you done to him, Cecily? Lewis was never like that before."

"Don't look at me. I didn't ask him to do any of that, but he's so eager."

"Now I'm really worried about what you've done to him." Sean sat down and picked up a pen. "Lewis has made it clear over the years that he's happy to remain a bachelor and he won't have children. Yet, he's helping you out and taking on a caretaking role. I'm getting really confused."

Cecily had been confused as well. When she moved in, Lewis had been quite vocal about being childfree. He didn't mind children being around him, but he preferred it if they mostly left him alone. And he had no desire to hold a baby. Cecily had found it a little strange that a man didn't want to have children, or even hold a baby, but she hadn't questioned it. It was something she could respect, even if she didn't understand it.

Now she had brought Oliver home, she was shocked at how much Lewis wanted to help her. He was willing to look after Oliver while she was working or if she needed to run a quick errand. There were even a couple of times when Cecily was desperate for sleep, and Lewis, with Emma's help, had taken Oliver away so she could sleep for a couple of hours. It had taken a while for Cecily to get her head around the fact that her childfree neighbor was helping her out. Even Emma was bewildered; she had confessed that finding a potential bride for Lewis was difficult as all the women she consulted wanted children, and they wouldn't choose Lewis as he didn't like children.

"I've given up trying to wonder what's going on in his head. I've never really understood him." Cecily picked up Oliver's cloth and wiped his mouth as he dribbled with a grin. "At least he's helping me out. My in-laws are too far away to actually help, and my own family seems to be content with sitting back and waiting for me to fail."

"They're still refusing to help with the newest addition to their family?" Sean snorted. "I knew Felicity was a bit of a witch, but that's just awful. Sorry, Cecily, I know that's your mother..."

"I've called her far worse in my head. That's tame compared to what I've thought." Cecily frowned. "It is really annoying that they won't help, and they're just waiting for me to show that I'm a bad mother before they swoop in and take Oliver away."

Sean didn't look happy hearing that. He shook his head and tapped the end of his pen on the desk.

"It would explain the rumors I've been hearing."

"What rumors?"

"That you're neglecting Oliver."

Cecily groaned. Not this again.

"I've been hearing those since I went home with Oliver. I know I made a mistake leaving him at the schoolhouse after giving birth, but I was in a bad place. I panicked."

"I'm not condoning you for leaving Oliver. You thought you were doing the right thing at the time, and you decided to keep him instead of giving him up for adoption. That's your prerogative."

"Not according to Mother and my brothers," Cecily said bitterly. "They still think I should give Oliver to them as they would never abandon him. I do feel guilty but I know he will be better off with me."

Sean rolled his eyes. "As if that lot knows how to raise a child. I look at you, and then I look at them, and I wonder how you are even related."

Cecily would take that as a compliment. Her brothers were nightmares, and they had been babied their whole lives. Her parents had a very feudal way of how a family worked. Cecily was not a son, so she was considered further down the pecking order. She was expected to cook, clean, and raise her younger brothers while her parents did whatever they wanted and spent their money on their sons. Cecily was lucky if she had anything paid for her, or if her parents remembered she was a member of the family.

Getting married was the only way to get out of the house, and she had been lucky to marry someone who loved her. Her parents hadn't been impressed, but they hadn't argued with their son-in-law; he had threatened to set them straight if they put a hand on his wife. Cecily had never had anyone stand up for her before that and it was a revelation. To be loved for who she was; she missed him so much.

"I think my parents wonder how I'm a member of the family." Cecily could feel her arms tightening around Oliver, which had him squawking a little. She loosened her hold a little, adjusting her son on her lap. "I know of the reports they've been spreading around town about how I'm a bad mother, how Oliver isn't looked after properly, and that I'm abusing him. I know they're false, and I know they started them, but it still gets to me. I'm their daughter, so why would they behave so badly towards me?"

"I doubt we'll ever find out. Sometimes, there never seems to be a reason for being horrible human beings." Sean gave her a gentle smile. "But, I can safely say that you're doing well with Oliver. He's growing nicely, he seems to be hitting his milestones, and I see no signs of abuse. With the support you've been getting from everyone, you've done a really good job."

"Thanks." Cecily grimaced as Oliver started to wriggle and get off her lap. "I'm not really looking forward to the mobile stage, though. He's starting to think about crawling."

"That's perfectly normal. But it's going to be the time for you to grow eyes in the back of your head." Sean chuckled as Oliver tried to fling himself back, almost falling out of Cecily's arms. "I'm glad he didn't do that while I was looking him over."

"Lucky you," Cecily muttered. She managed to get Oliver upright, although from his whining he wasn't happy. "I can see him getting into everything. Then I'll be paranoid that he's going to get hurt."

"He's a baby. It's perfectly natural. And you'll be fine." Sean's eyes twinkled. "I'm sure Lewis will be able to help out more. He might not like children, but he prefers them to be mobile if he had to be around them, so that might work in your favor."

"You're making it sound like I should use my son to charm him, Sean."

"You never know. Women have done it before."

Cecily rolled her eyes with a smile. "Ever the cynic, aren't you?"

"Considering how many ladies Emma's brought to Lubbock with children, or how many children have been involved, it'll be a surprise if children weren't the catalyst for many of the marriages."

"Someone sounds bitter," she said with a chuckle

"What makes you think I'm bitter?"

Cecily bit her tongue on that. She knew the reason why. Even when she was mostly incapacitated and faint from blood loss, she had noticed the chemistry between Sean and the nursemaid, Molly. It was clear that there were strong feelings on both sides, but they seemed intent on ignoring them. Especially Sean.

It did make her wonder what Sean was so scared of that made him stop short of actually saying something about it. From the way she looked at him, Molly really wanted him to. Cecily was surprised she hadn't said anything herself.

Those two were daft. She liked both of them, but they were just fools ignoring their feelings.

"I'm glad you don't believe the lies about me, Sean." Cecily jerked her head away as Oliver threw his head back, missing her jaw but hitting her collar bone. That hurt. "My parents have been known to take even the smartest people in before."

"Cecily, I've kept a close eye on you for months since you and Oliver came here, and I'm confident that you two are going to be fine. Those who are stupid enough to listen to gossip will see it was all lies, in time."

"I hope so. I don't want to explain myself for the tenth time in a day when someone confronts me about it."

"People are doing that?"

"Sadly. Mostly Mother's friends." Cecily shook her head. "It's driving me mad."

"Just ignore them. What they think doesn't matter." Sean watched as Oliver threw himself backward again. "I think someone's due for a nap. He looks like he's about to throw a tantrum."

"He normally does this when he starts to get tired." Cecily looked around at her things scattered across the settee. "This is going to be fun."

"I'll give you a hand." Sean scribbled something on his notepad. "Just don't tell Molly that I did. She'll start teasing me about softening towards children."

Cecily laughed. "There's nothing wrong with being soft with children."

Sean grunted. "Not when I'm involved, trust me."

Cecily smiled but she didn't know what he meant by that.

CHAPTER TWO

Lewis found himself glancing towards the door again, and then realized what he was doing. Cecily said she wouldn't be too long at the surgery, and not to worry about her. Yet here he was, wondering if they were all right and how Oliver was getting on. Did Sean believe the lies about Cecily being a bad mother? If he did, he wasn't the man Lewis thought he was.

You really need to stop thinking of her as if she's your woman. She's your neighbor, nothing more.

That's easier said than done.

The moment Cecily and her husband had moved into the house next door, Lewis knew he was going to be jealous that someone had managed to snag a sweet, gentle woman like Cecily. She was just adorable, a little timid but she had slowly been coming out of her shell and gaining her confidence. Considering who her family was, it was no surprise that she was painfully shy. Normally, a woman like that would be someone he kept his distance from, but Lewis had always been weak for ladies with red hair. Add to that those gorgeous green eyes, and he could understand why her husband had married her.

It was a shame their marriage hadn't lasted long. Lewis could see the two of them being married until they were old and gray, but now that wasn't going to happen. Cecily had been through some rough times, becoming a widow and then being a single mother. It had been hard on her but she was tougher than she thought, and Lewis had been surprised by her strength.

That just made him admire her even more. Cecily Campbell was one of a kind.

If only he could stop looking out for her like a lovesick fool. It was beginning to get embarrassing.

"You're doing it again."

Lewis turned and saw Christian giving him a knowing look.

"What am I doing?"

"Staring at the door. You've done that a dozen times since Cecily went to the surgery."

"I haven't done it a dozen times."

"Close enough." Christian gestured at the printing plate close to Lewis. "You're supposed to be finishing that compositing, to make sure it is ready for pressing. You'd better concentrate, to make sure it is done properly and doesn't get ruined."

"I am." Lewis looked down at the plate. The words had to be done in reverse so that they were then inked and placed into the Washington Press he had. It was then slid into the press and the pressure applied and it printed onto the paper. Preparing the plate took a lot of concentration and looking at it he had a word wrong. Gunfight would actually print as gufnight.

Glancing across at Christian, he could see him chuckling. Lewis swapped the letters and placed the plate inside the press. Quickly, he inked the plate and replaced the cover, sliding it into the press and then pulling down the handle. That done he opened it up again and pointed at the paper. "See? It's printing correctly, and I am keeping an eye on it."

Christian grunted.

"This is your business, Lewis. It's your machine and your livelihood. I shouldn't be telling you what to do."

Lewis sighed. His brother meant well, but there were times when he wished his older brother would just trust him. He had been printing since he was eighteen, taking over the business at thirty, and he knew exactly what he was doing. True, he did need an assistant permanently and not an occasional helper in his brother, who kept forgetting that Lewis was meant to be in charge.

He wouldn't have needed Lewis' help today if Cecily was around. She was often around giving him a hand most days with Oliver in his Moses basket or strapped to her chest. Having her in the workshop was certainly easier on the eye than his at times annoying brother.

"Honestly, Lewis, you're such a sap." Christian took out the sheet he had printed and put it aside before picking out another two sheets. He was a large man, a little overweight and the work was hard for him. Wiping his sweating forehead he lowered the lid of the press again.

"I've never seen you go barmy about a woman before, especially not a woman with a child. You said you would never have a child in your life."

"I'm not barmy over Cecily."

Christian snorted. "I know you are. I've been in your life since you came into the world, and I know when you feel something so strongly."

Lewis was glad he was feeling hot and sweaty already - his red cheeks from the heat hid his blushing. Christian knew him too well.

"I didn't plan on having feelings like this for my neighbor. And she was married when she moved in, so it just feels wrong that I feel anything at all. As for Oliver..." Lewis started working on the pate for the next page. "I know I'm not a person who feels comfortable around children, but I can make an exception for him. He's a little cutie."

Christian shook his head.

"This is coming from someone who refused to hold my children when they were born and keeps his nieces and nephews at arm's length. Now you're looking for any opportunity to hold Oliver. If I didn't know how you felt about Mrs. Campbell, I certainly would with the amount of time you have her son in your arms."

Lewis winced. "I didn't realize I was that obvious."

"More than obvious. If I didn't love you and know what you're like, I'd be rather insulted."

"As if you get insulted over anything." Christian shrugged.

"It depends on the situation; sure, it takes a lot to get me riled up. What's different about Cecily and her son compared to everyone else?"

Lewis wasn't sure he could answer this question. It was probably the red hair if he really had to think about it. That made him stop and stare, certainly. Gradually, Lewis had realized there was more to her, even if she was so shy. She was a sweet, endearing young woman, and she was working really hard to look after her son. There was a character there that he couldn't put his finger on and she was just so easy to talk to. Everything felt better if he shared it with her.

"You're a real sap, Lewis."

"Would you stop calling me that?"

"Well, you are." Christian chuckled as he wiped the sweat from his forehead. "And I thought I was daft when I met my wife. I know I was a real fool around her. Never did I think it would happen to you, or that you would be falling for a woman with a baby."

"I didn't think that would happen, either." Lewis could feel the sweat burning his eyes and he tried to blink it away. "And here I was thinking I would be alone for the rest of my life as women always want children. Emma had told me the other day that there wasn't anything she could do if the women who wrote to her said they wanted to have a family. Apparently, just a husband doesn't count as family."

"What's wrong with children, exactly?"

Lewis gave his brother a pointed look. "Do you remember our childhood and what happened there?"

Christian sighed. "I haven't forgotten, but knowing how bad our childhood was made me determined to be a better father. It's not stopped me from wanting children."

"Well, it stopped me."

"You think you're going to be as bad as Father?"

Lewis didn't answer, concentrating on his work while trying not to stare at the door looking for Cecily. He didn't think he would be as bad as their Father. That man had neglected them and then shouted and hit them when he was around. He lost his temper over the slightest things. Lewis knew he wasn't like that — but there was always that fear in his head, what if he was? His father's words that he would never be good enough were always at the back of his mind.

Christian kept telling him they were going to be different, that they could make sure they didn't make the same mistakes, but Lewis didn't want to take that chance. Also, after helping Christian raise their younger siblings, now adults who were a little insufferable, he wasn't keen on raising children.

That was until he saw Oliver. He was enough to soften anyone. Then again, he did have a mother Lewis would do anything for.

Christian was right. He was a sap.

"Just be careful being around Cecily," his brother warned as he stepped away from his printing press, taking out a handkerchief to wipe his face and neck. Christian did look like he had been stuck in a steam hut for several hours. "She's had a tough upbringing, and she's raising a child alone. She won't want to be messed around with again."

Lewis stiffened.

"I'm not going to mess her around."

"You'd better not. She won't be tolerant of you if you do that."

Lewis snorted. "She's special, Christian. I wouldn't do that to her at all. Why are you so sure that I will?"

"Because I know you." Christian pushed his handkerchief back into his pocket. "The novelty of looking after a baby is going to wear off eventually, and you'll want out. After your adamant responses about becoming a father for years, I don't think you'll last long."

"I thought you would be supportive, happy that I've found someone I could spend my life with."

"One, you haven't told her. You've been dancing around the subject for the last six months. And two, she has a child. You didn't want to be a father, and yet you'd become a stepfather. How is that a different role?"

Lewis glared at his brother. "I'm taking things slowly, Christian. Leave me alone on it."

"Someone's got to nudge you along."

"You sound like you're scolding me."

Christian spread his hands. "If it gets through to you. Cecily's a pretty woman. I'm sure once she's ready to marry again, she'll be going for someone who's actually proactive and isn't using her son as a way to win her over."

Lewis glared at him. "I'm not using Oliver to win her over. That's not fair."

"Are you not? Any woman would be at your feet if you fawned over their child."

"At least I accept Oliver. He's a sweet baby."

"I agree on that." Christian's mouth twitched. "I never thought I'd hear of you changing a diaper. What happened to my child-hating brother?"

"He grew up."

"Sure he did." Christian's smile began to fade. "I just hope you don't change your mind about this further down the line. Cecily Campbell's a lovely lady. She doesn't deserve to have you walk out on her because you can't cut being a stepfather."

Lewis scowled. "That's not going to happen."

He would never do that. The idea of becoming a stepfather had given him pause. But he knew that he could do it, and he had come around to the idea. It wouldn't be easy, but life was never easy.

And it would be worth it if Cecily came along with the baby.

He just needed to get over his nerves - they just wouldn't go away when she was around - and tell her how he really felt. Lewis had never been uncertain of himself with women, so this was concerning and annoying. All he wanted to do was just tell her.

It was not that easy with the insecurities in the back of his mind.

"It had better not happen, Lewis. Because you'll ruin more than just one life if this goes wrong." Christian then flapped his arms at his brother. "Now, you go outside and get some air. I'll finish off here."

"I thought I was the boss in here."

"True, but you're getting distracted. You might as well go and look for her."

Lewis growled. "I'm not distracted."

"Maybe not, but you won't be calm until you see her. So get lost and go find her. You're making me nervous."

Lewis watched as his brother switched the sheets around, putting the fresh prints on the pile he had been compiling. For someone who was as wide as a tree trunk - and just about as solid as one - Christian had a speed about him that Lewis envied. It certainly helped while he was working.

"What was it like when you fell in love with Amanda?"

"You mean, was I a coward who took forever to tell her?"

"That's not what I meant…"

"I know what you meant." Christian smiled at him. "But yes, I was a coward. I thought she was too good for me. Someone like her deserved better. And when I finally confessed how I felt, I found out she felt the same way. Then I felt like I was the greatest person in the world. Things are a lot lighter after a confession like that."

"But you understand how unnerving it can be to experience it for the first time."

"Of course. And I know moping around isn't going to make anything progress. You need to tell her before someone else comes along and takes her away. Then you really will be left alone." Christian looked up as the sound of a baby crying filled the workshop. "Sounds like they've returned. Maybe you should go and see your neighbors. It might be a good time to tell her."

Lewis didn't know about that. But he was already heading towards the door.

"You can manage on your own for a while, can't you?"

"How long have I helped you out? You don't need to ask." Christian waved him away. "Just go away and be a fool elsewhere."

CHAPTER THREE

 ecily was relieved when she finally arrived home. Oliver was getting more agitated each moment, the poor mite was tired. It was typical that he started grumbling when she had him alone and they weren't at home. Still, at six months old, he got tired pretty quickly, it was understandable.

At least he had behaved himself with the doctor. Oliver wasn't too keen on many men, so he had a tendency to lash out. Then again, Sean probably wouldn't bat an eyelid if he did get kicked in the face; he was just so calm and always seemed to know what to do.

He and Lewis were the only two Oliver didn't act out with. Surprisingly, he was calm with the doctor and the printer. Even though the latter was the man who said he didn't want children and wasn't too keen on them when they were around.

Cecily still wondered about that. Lewis had said he was someone who kept his distance from children until they were a little older. He preferred them when they needed minimal care so he could put them off in a corner and ignore them. And yet, when Cecily came home with Oliver, he was the one to hold him as she got herself settled, and at times, he seemed reluctant to let him go.

Had he changed his mind? Cecily had no idea what was going on with him, but she wasn't about to argue; she was grateful for any help.

If only my heart didn't miss a beat whenever he's around. The treacherous thing shouldn't do that.

She pushed those thoughts aside. She would not think about how her feelings for her neighbor and employer had shifted. That wasn't going to help anyone, least of all her. Even if he had softened towards Oliver, there was no hope that he would have a more permanent role in their lives. Cecily knew she shouldn't get her hopes up, she had to be realistic. And yet, when she was in his company, she found herself wanting more than just a friend.

She was mad. She was supposed to be grieving the loss of her husband, not thinking about another man. The way her pulse raced in his presence made her feel a little guilty.

Hopefully, her husband wouldn't mind that she was having feelings for someone so soon. He wouldn't want her left alone, not with her family waiting to pounce. To tell everyone she was a bad mother. They wanted to take Oliver from her, and he wouldn't have wanted her to face that alone.

Cecily thought about her family and shuddered. Especially her mother. Felicity had been trying to get the sheriffs to take Oliver away, saying he was being hurt and neglected. Even Jake was getting fed up with the conversations.

Why couldn't they just leave her alone?

Oliver was getting fussier as she climbed the stairs and went into her bedroom. With a smile, she put him down in his cot and gave him his favorite toy. Oliver calmed down a little, but he was still upset. She had fed him before going to Sean, so he wasn't hungry and he was dry. But he was very tired, and the little thing was fighting it off.

Cecily could feel a headache coming on. It was at moments like this that she felt she wasn't cut out to be a mother. She had done everything, and she knew she was doing it right, but Oliver was still unhappy. It hurt her heart and made her doubt her own abilities.

It was going to be a while before he fell asleep.

"Cecily?"

Cecily gasped and spun around. The tall, fair-haired figure in the doorway was almost a welcoming sight. Then she realized that he was actually in the house, almost in her bedroom!

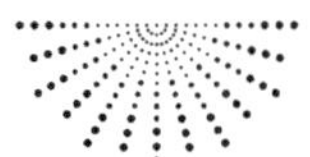

CHAPTER FOUR

"*L*ewis! How did you get in? I didn't hear you knocking."

"You left the front door open."

"I did?"

"I'm afraid so. I called, but I don't think you heard." Lewis nodded at the cot. "I take it he's overtired."

Cecily winced. "I'm really sorry about the noise. I didn't mean to disturb you."

"Not at all." Lewis entered the room. "Why don't I get him to sleep? You go and take a moment downstairs."

"You... you will..."

"You look like you're about to drop yourself. Why don't you go and sit down and I'll stay with him until he drops off?"

Cecily was still trying to get the words to sink in. Even though Lewis had been helping her for the last few months, since she came back from the surgery, it was still a shock when he offered to help. It made her wonder what his ulterior motive was, but when she asked what he wanted, Lewis simply brushed it off and said it was about neighbors helping each other out.

Why did she think that there was more going on?

"Are you sure about this?" Cecily looked down at Oliver, who was still crying and chewing on his fists. "What can you do that I can't?"

"I'm sure, and I think you need to focus on yourself. You can't look after a child when you look about to drop. Maybe he can pick up on your exhaustion and it's stressing him."

That made sense and she nodded.

Lewis took her arm and steered her towards the door. "Just go and sit downstairs. You've done your bit. Let me help."

Cecily knew she should be arguing - this was her son, after all - but she allowed Lewis to urge her out of the room. She hesitated in the doorway, watching as he went to the cot and leaned over, giving Oliver a smile that made her pulse stumble.

Oliver seemed to calm down a little, but not much. Then Lewis started talking in a low voice, the rumble barely reaching Cecily. The whining stopped and she heard Oliver chuckle. It was working!

Cecily decided to trust Lewis and leave him to it. He was pretty good at calming Oliver down, although how he did it when he told everyone how much he disliked small children, she had no idea. It was bewildering.

Could he be wanting more from you? Could there be a chance of a future? Cecily shook the thoughts away, they were too confusing to contemplate. She was just clutching for a lifeline, these feelings could not be real.

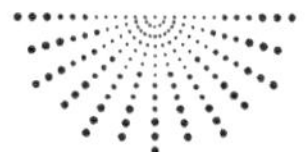

CHAPTER FIVE

Stumbling a little on the stairs, she settled in the living room. It was getting a little warmer outside, but not by much. The fire was empty, and the room had a distinct chill. Maybe she should think about laying the fire and getting herself warm. Did she have enough firewood? It wouldn't take long, but Cecily was feeling so very tired that she couldn't muster the energy to try. That had been happening a lot lately.

Pulling a blanket over her she curled up on the sofa. Closing her eyes for a moment wouldn't do any harm, would it?

The next thing Cecily knew was someone was gently shaking her awake. Blinking, she became aware that she was lying down, the blanket tucked around her, and the fire was burning brightly. It certainly hadn't been laid when she closed her eyes. Had she fallen asleep?

Lewis was kneeling by the sofa. He gave her a smile.

"Oliver's going to be wanting something to eat soon."

"Oh. Right." It took a moment for Cecily to realize what he had just said. "How long have I been asleep?"

"About three hours. I got him to sleep pretty quickly and then I found you fast asleep. I didn't want you to get cold; the weather is still not great right now."

Cecily looked at the fire. Had she been that exhausted that she hadn't heard him moving around?

"I didn't realize I was that tired."

"Sometimes, it just hits you. And you have been busy with Oliver lately."

"How did you get him to sleep?"

Lewis winked. "I have my ways." He shifted to sit on the edge of the sofa. "How was the visit with Sean? Is Oliver well?"

"Very well." Cecily managed to sit up. "Sean's not concerned about anything. In fact, he seemed very happy with Oliver's progress."

"That's something."

Cecily made a face. "At least we can put those awful rumors to bed. I hate having people stare at me because they believe the lies my family has told."

"Anyone looking at Oliver can see he's looked after, and he's happy. They can go suck on a lemon, as far as I'm concerned."

Cecily couldn't help but giggle. "Suck on a lemon. Where did you get that from?"

"One of Christian's nephews keeps saying it. I don't know where he heard it, but it seems to be his favorite phrase." Lewis' expression softened. "You're looking more rested. That's something."

"I'm sorry I left you looking after Oliver. I know you have to work..."

"I'm willing to help you out when I can. But it will mean that you have to work extra to make up for it."

"I promise I'll do that." Cecily bit her lip. "I do feel awful for it, though. I'm meant to be the parent..."

"And even a parent needs a break. I'm happy to help." Lewis touched her knee. "Don't fret so much, Cecily. You know I'm always going to help."

Cecily knew that. Even with Lewis' declarations when they first met, he would always help her out. But she still felt like she was asking for too much. He wasn't a parent, he was a neighbor. True, neighbors did help each other out, but not to this extent. Was she taking too much from him? Would it push him away?

That thought drove a fear into her heart that was hard to understand.

Cecily tried to push the fear down. There was no way she should rely on Lewis this much, maybe it was time to pull away from him. If this was to end eventually, it would be best to break it off before she got too involved.

"You're thinking again," Lewis said.

"Sorry?"

"I can see things turning." Lewis tapped the side of his head. "What's wrong, Cecily? You know you can talk to me."

Cecily knew that, but even then she felt the words getting stuck in her throat. *Why are you helping me so much?* That's what she really wanted to ask, but she couldn't do it. She just couldn't.

She was distracted from her thoughts when she heard a familiar female voice outside. Moments later, it was joined by a male voice, one that sounded like it was about to scold. Then the female voice got louder.

Cecily groaned. She didn't need this right now.

"It's Mother. She's here."

"And it sounds like she's having a standoff with Christian." Lewis stood up. "You stay here. We'll make her leave."

"I'm not sitting here while you do that." Throwing the blanket aside, Cecily stood up. "She's my mother. I'll deal with her."

"Are you sure?"

"Yes."

Lewis didn't look convinced, but he nodded and stepped aside. "All right. But I'm not going anywhere."

Cecily hoped that was true.

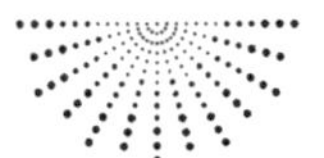

ewis wasn't keen on Cecily going to confront her mother; there were times when he wished she would stand up to the woman more than she did. Even in a case like this, it was hard to stay strong when you had a woman like Felicity Tamberi on a tirade. She was one of those people who expected to be obeyed no matter what.

Felicity had grown up as a member of the wealthy elite eventually becoming a member of the Tamberi family. It meant she ended up expecting to get her way no matter what, Lewis couldn't tolerate that behavior. Cecily didn't like it, either, but she was more tired of her family and frustrated and a little scared that they would get their way. Lewis was still trying to figure out how a mother and daughter could be so different.

He followed Cecily outside and found Christian squaring up to a woman in her late forties with faded red hair and a statuesque frame. The clothes she was wearing would probably have cost him a month's work. Though she was a fine-looking woman, it was like looking at Cecily in twenty-five years.

It was a shame that the woman's attitude and demeanor were so different.

"You are not going inside, Mrs. Tamberi." Christian stood in front of Felicity, his huge arms folded as he scowled at her. "Cecily and Oliver are resting."

"That is my daughter's house, and I have every right to go in if I want to." Felicity snapped. "Now get out of the way."

"I was present when Cecily told you not to visit again. I'm merely respecting her wishes until she tells me otherwise."

Felicity snorted rudely. "You big oaf. Get out of my way. Or do you want me to call the sheriff?"

Lewis could see Christian was handling it. Still, the last thing he wanted was Felicity actually getting into the house. He stayed by the door, closing it behind him, as Cecily stalked down the path towards her mother. Her hands were clenched, and Lewis could see the tension in her shoulders.

"What are you doing here, Mother? I told you not to come back unless you were ready to apologize."

Her mother turned to her. "Apologize for what?"

"For telling everyone that I'm a bad mother. For giving the sheriff false reports about me." Cecily put her hands on her hips. "For trying to kidnap Oliver when I was recovering from his birth. Do you want me to go on?"

"Kidnap?" Felicity rolled her eyes. "How is what I tried to do kidnapping? I was merely looking out for my grandson's safety. You did abandon him."

"That doesn't mean you could waltz in and try to take him!"

"If you will leave your son outside a schoolhouse..."
Cecily let out a growl that made everyone jump.

Lewis hadn't heard her get that upset before. He watched as she stepped towards her mother.

"That was a mistake," Cecily said, standing tall, her shoulders squared and looking her mother in the eyes. "I was hurt. If you were in my position, I'm sure you would have panicked as well. But that's not happening anymore. Oliver stays with me."

Felicity scoffed. "I don't think so. You can't look after yourself, so how can you possibly look after a baby."

"I've been doing fine for six months. And my neighbors have helped." Cecily nodded at Christian. "I'm doing fine, and I would be doing better if I had the support of my family."

"Well, you don't!"

"Why is that, I wonder?" Cecily shook her head but kept a confident stance. "Because I married for love and not for your advantage? Because I stayed in this house? Because I'm not allowing for you to order me about like I'm one of the servants?"

Lewis watched as the older woman's nostrils flared. Cecily had hit nearer to the mark than she expected.

He had heard stories that the Tamberi family favored the men and that the women were often neglected or treated worse if they wouldn't do as they were told. Felicity Tamberi seemed to be a driving force behind it all. Lewis had known a few older members of the Tamberi family from his childhood before Felicity married into the family, and they had been wealthy but never to the extent they were now. Then, they had been different, separate, but this... there was an archaic attitude in this woman.

He felt sorry for Cecily having to deal with this woman as a mother.

"You are a Tamberi, Cecily," Felicity said tightly. "And we look after our own. But we can't do that if you fight back and rebel. Is that how a mother is supposed to behave?"

"How am I rebelling, Mother? Because I married someone I loved?"

"We know what's best for you, and we can clearly see that you're not fit to be a mother. You're not the right sort."

Christian barked out a laugh. "The right sort? What on earth does that mean?"

"I wasn't talking to you, so you can leave. I will have my daughter back with me today. Just you wait and see." Turning her gaze on Cecily. "Cecily, come with me now!"

Cecily felt her heart miss a beat and her treacherous feet started to move toward her mother. It was a natural reaction after a lifetime of living with this woman.

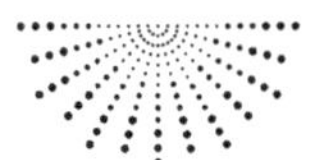

CHAPTER SEVEN

Fighting down her panic and her feelings of insecurity, Cecily stopped and stood her ground. "Christian is not going anywhere, Mother, and neither am I." Cecily held up a hand to Christian. "And you need to explain why I'm not the right sort to raise a child."

Felicity's eyes narrowed. "You know exactly what I mean."

"How so? Because I'm really confused."

"This is not the conversation we should be having outside, Cecily. We should go indoors. Away from..." Felicity gestured at Christian and glared at Lewis... "people not in the family. This is none of their business."

Lewis didn't like hearing that. He pushed off the door and headed towards the middle-aged woman.

"In what way is this none of my business?" he demanded. "I've helped Cecily look after your grandson since she came home with him. I've seen him more than you have because I don't judge Cecily to your very high and unrealistic expectations. She's done a great job and Oliver is doing really well. In spite of what you believe, there is no need for you to keep charging in and saying Cecily is a bad mother. That is just spiteful... you should be proud of her for managing all this while she's grieving the loss of her husband."

From the look on Felicity's face, she didn't like being talked back to. Cecily glanced at Lewis and gave him a slight shake of her head. She wanted him to step back, but Lewis was not having it. This was not right.

"I think you need to stay out of family business, sir," Felicity said icily. "You're not Cecily's husband, and you're not Tamberi. So you should keep your opinions to yourself."

"I don't think so. Cecily's told you that you can have a relationship with Oliver if you would stop accusing her of being a bad parent. And we know it's you spreading the rumors around Lubbock about her neglecting Oliver and how she's going mad." Lewis folded his arms. "That's not going to endear yourself to your daughter, is it? Just because you're not getting your own way it doesn't mean you get to be horrible to your own child!"

"Lewis!" Cecily grabbed his arm. "Stop now! Go back inside and make sure Oliver's all right, will you?"

Lewis didn't want to go. Not when Felicity was still present. But the look in her eyes told him to stop. This was her fight, not his, and she wanted to do it alone. Lewis didn't want her to be alone, though. He needed to be there.

"Lewis," Cecily pleaded quietly. "Please."

She had said that magic word. Lewis knew he couldn't do anything but comply. He wanted to stay and be on Cecily's side - especially against a woman like Felicity - but he couldn't fight when she was begging him to focus on Oliver.

Reluctantly, he stepped away and headed into the house. Christian was still there. He could keep an eye on the old battleax. Lewis would rather it was him, but Christian was the next best thing. As far as he was concerned, Felicity was not coming into the house.

Lewis went upstairs and into Cecily's room. Oliver was still asleep, tucked under his blanket and cuddling his toy. He looked so sweet and innocent right now. It was hard not to soften seeing this beautiful child.

He sat on the bed and watched the cot, seeing Oliver's chest rise and fall with his breathing. How could anyone accuse Cecily of hurting this boy? She clearly loved her son, even after the shaky start.

Felicity had to be mad to think it was all right to accuse her daughter in such a way. What could she hope to achieve? The thought that Cecily would come back and hand over the baby to her after this was ludicrous!

Lewis prayed that he was right. That Cecily would stay strong and stay away from that evil family.

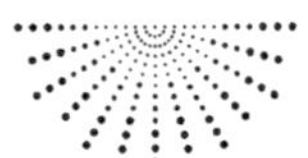

Felicity sneered at Lewis's retreating back as he disappeared into the house.

"He's a bit too invested in you, Cecily."

Cecily bristled. "He's my neighbor and he's given me a job, Mother. He's allowed to be concerned."

"That is not what I meant. Is there something going on between you two?"

"Certainly not! I've got more important things to worry about."

Felicity scoffed. "At this point in time, I don't believe you. Not with the way he looks at you. I'd say he's looking to build his own happy family."

Christian snorted. "Come off it. Lewis doesn't even like children. Why would he marry someone with a baby?"

Even though Cecily knew that was true, that statement didn't sit well with her. Shoving the feeling of nausea aside, she focused on Felicity. Why wouldn't the woman just leave?

"Mother, I don't know what you're trying to do, but I made my conditions clear when you first tried to see Oliver."

"I remember. And I don't think you should be giving conditions to your mother about your child."

"You tried to kidnap him when I was recovering!"

Felicity rolled her eyes.

"I did nothing of the sort. I was the grandmother trying to look after my grandbaby until you were well enough to come home."

"No, you were looking to take him away. If you had succeeded, I would never get him back. I know how these things work with you, Mother. You never do things in the best interest of anyone else. It's always what you want."

Felicity's eyes glinted dangerously. "You presume a lot of me, Cecily."

"And I would be right."

"Just as I would be right to say that you are not fit to be a mother."

"Why?" Cecily demanded. "Because I'm a widow now? Because I had a moment of panic? Or because you want to bring me back into the family and punish me for 'straying'?"

"You are too suspicious, Cecily. The family is supposed to help each other."

Cecily snorted. "Family. You never cared about me. My brothers were always favored over me, and I was left alone or treated like I was one of the servants. How can I call anyone who treated me like that family?"

"Everyone has a place in a family."

"And you had mine at the bottom of the pecking order! If you didn't make it clear with that, you made it clear with the way you treated me. I'm not going back to that, and I will not have Oliver growing up in that environment. I understand that he's your first grandchild, that you've been waiting for my brothers to marry and have children of their own, but Oliver will not be a substitute until that happens."

Something flickered in Felicity's eyes, and Cecily knew she had hit the nail on the head. This was what it was all about. Oliver was the first grandchild, and they wanted him back in among the family. They were no doubt hoping that they would keep him permanently away from Cecily.

That was not going to happen.

"Why don't we go inside and talk?" Felicity started to walk around her daughter towards the house. "We can discuss things in a more adult way if we sit down."

"You're not going inside." Cecily grabbed her mother's arm. "My husband told you that he wouldn't permit you in the house, and I stand by that. Nobody goes inside unless I allow it."

Felicity's face was turning as red as her hair. She looked down at Cecily's hand on her arm.

"Let go of me, Cecily," she said tightly. "You have no right to put your hands on me."

"And you have no right to assume that you can just ignore what I've been saying to you since I got married and do whatever you want. I'm not having you in my house, and I won't let you see Oliver if you're going to keep accusing me of neglect."

"I have a right to express my concerns." Felicity yanked her arm away. "I am a grandmother now."

"It's not expressing concerns. It's you saying that you're going to make my life a misery until I come back and do as I'm told. If anything was wrong with Oliver, I would have been arrested a long time ago." Cecily stepped between her mother and the house. "Just go home. You're not welcome here. Unless you are going to give me a genuine apology about what you've done, both in the past and now, I don't want to see you."

Felicity reeled back like she had been slapped.

"You can't mean that."

"I do mean it. You're my mother, yes, but it doesn't mean I bow down to what you say. And after what you've done going around spreading lies about my parenting, I think it's easier for me to keep you away."

Her mother looked shocked. Her mouth opened and closed.

"You... you can't keep me away!"

"I've been doing that since Oliver was born when I found out what you tried to do. How can I trust you not to do that again, Mother? You've shown that I can't trust you to buy a toy for him, never mind being in the same room as him! Besides," Cecily went on as she advanced on her mother, feeling a smidgen of satisfaction that Felicity started backing up, "it's my duty as a mother to protect my child from outside influences that could be considered dangerous to him, and that includes my own family."

Cecily had no idea where she had gotten this confidence from. She had never done this before. In the past, her tactics had been simply running away and locking herself in the house. Felicity was tenacious, and Cecily knew it would wear her down if she kept pushing her. The thought of going back to a family that degraded her and treated her like less than nothing wasn't appealing at all. Cecily knew if she went back that she would be married off and she would barely see her son again. That was not happening.

"Go home, Mother." Cecily turned away and headed towards the house. "Christian, would you make sure Tamberi leaves in an orderly fashion? If not, I'm sure Sheriff Hutchinson will have a good time removing her."

Christian grinned and nodded his head. "It will be my pleasure, Cecily."

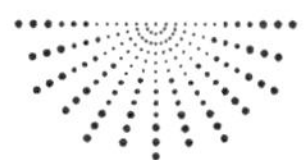

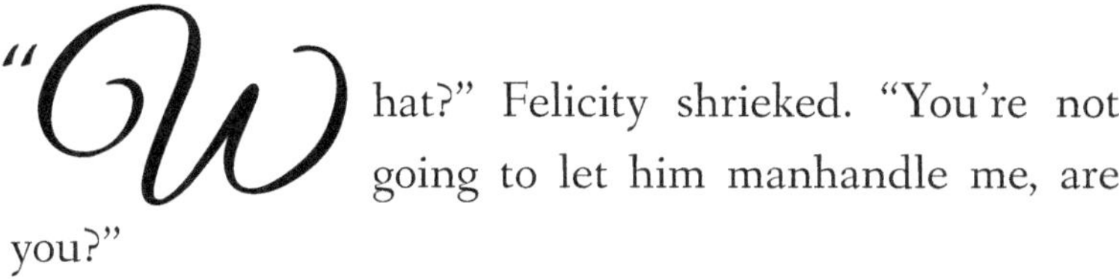

"hat?" Felicity shrieked. "You're not going to let him manhandle me, are you?"

"Leave right now, and that won't happen." Cecily barely looked back as she opened the door. "Good day, Mrs. Tamberi, please don't come back here again."

Cecily maintained her speed and deportment until she got into the house and shut the door behind her. Leaning against it, she let the shakes come as she heard her mother shouting at Christian. Cecily knew if she had stayed out there any longer, she would have either tried to make a compromise that her mother didn't deserve or end up smacking her. Or possibly both. Right now, she was too tired to deal with this.

"Cecily?"

Cecily looked up. Lewis was coming down the stairs. The sight of him made her feel a little better, although it didn't ease the headache that was starting to build.

"How's Oliver?"

"He still hasn't woken up. What's going on out there?"

"I think Mother wants to see her grandson." Cecily rested her head against the door and closed her eyes. "She seems to think she still has a right even after all she's done. Refusing to let her see Oliver hasn't given her a hint that I want nothing to do with her."

"She still has the idea that she can get what she wants."

"You mean she still wants control?"

"Pretty much." The sound of Felicity shrieking reached their ears. "That sounds like Christian's had enough of her."

"What is he doing now?"

"He's probably slung her over his shoulder to carry her away. My brother's known for doing that when someone doesn't listen to reason."

Cecily couldn't help it, she was pleased to have such good friends. To have people around her now that she could lean on. It should be her family but it didn't matter, in many ways, Christian and Lewis were more like family to her than her own had ever been.

"Cecily?"

Lewis's touch on her arms had Cecily opening her eyes. He was standing right in front of her, his expression pressed into a frown as his eyes searched her face. She managed a small smile.

"I'll be fine. It's nothing I can't handle."

"She's going to keep coming back until she gets her own way."

"Not with me, Lewis. She did that to me for many years. She may be the matriarch of the Tamberi family, but she's not in charge of me, not anymore." Cecily shook her head. "I'm not going back, and until she admits that she's done wrong and repents for it, she's not going to see Oliver. I won't give her a chance to snatch him away from me."

Lewis nodded. "I understand. But do you want me to go to her? Maybe I could talk to her..."

"What could you do differently from what I've done, Lewis?"

"I don't know, but I'm sure I can think of something."

Cecily didn't think so. She shook her head.

"Thank you for the offer, but this is my fight. It's best that you leave it to me."

Lewis looked as if he didn't like that response. But he nodded, even as he scowled.

"I still don't like how she treats you." He shook his head. "It's laughable that she thinks you can play happy families after this."

"That's my mother for you. She dances to her own songs, most of which nobody's heard of before." Cecily touched his chest. "But thank you for offering. Just... just let me deal with Mother. It's my responsibility, nobody else's."

"Even so..."

"Please, Lewis?"

Lewis's lips tightened as he nodded.

"All right. I won't interfere but I'm here if you need me."

Those words filled her with warmth. The fact that he would trust her enough to handle this was a great boost to her confidence and knowing he was always there... that just made her feel good. It made her feel safe, secure... that there might be a future!

Her headache was getting worse. She leaned her head on his chest and his arms curled around her.

"Is your head beginning to hurt again?"

"I've been getting a lot of headaches lately. They're driving me mad." Cecily closed her eyes. "Do you need to go back to work immediately?"

"Not immediately." She felt Lewis stroking her back. "Take your time. I'll be here for you."

That was the best thing Cecily had heard all day.

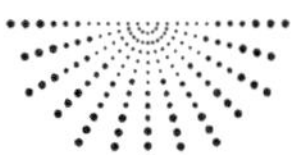

CHAPTER TEN

Lewis stood in the doorway and watched Cecily sleep. She had fallen asleep in his arms a short while ago, and he had managed to carry her up and tuck her into bed. She barely stirred as Lewis put her in the bed and then lifted a stirring Oliver from his cot. The baby was waking up, and he really needed his diaper changed. He was wriggling, not too happy with his current state.

Lewis knew he should be waking Cecily up and getting her to look after her son, but he didn't have the heart to do so. She had been emotionally drained from the confrontation with her mother, and it had given her a headache that seemed to wipe her out. After interacting with Felicity on several occasions, Lewis understood exactly how she felt. The woman was exhausting for anyone.

Cecily needed her rest and he wouldn't wake her.

Oliver was getting fussy, so he headed downstairs and focused on the little boy. A diaper was changed, Oliver was fed, and then Lewis took him out into the backyard. It was still afternoon, and it wasn't as cold as it had been earlier. A bit of fresh air would do them wonders.

Lewis walked around the garden, distracting Oliver with the various flowers and pointing out people who walked by on the other side of the fence. Several of the passers-by waved at him, and Oliver ended up attempting to wave back, which did look like he was fanning himself. It was really adorable.

Who wouldn't fall in love with a sweetie like this lad?

That gave Lewis pause for thought. When had he started loving Oliver like his own? That had just crept up on him. Lewis had memories of his childhood that weren't good. He had barely had a proper childhood, his parents always forcing him and Christian to raise their younger siblings while they worked. The problem was, his parents didn't want to be parents as soon as they got home. It was all left to Lewis and Christian.

After having siblings depend on him when he wanted to be with his friends, and now they were still trying to rely on him like they had no idea how to be independent, Lewis had vowed he would never have children. They were too much hassle and there was too big a chance that he would mess them up like he was. Christian could get past it and have his own big family, but he had always wanted a family of his own. He was a good father and good husband.

Lewis had no qualms about remaining a bachelor for the rest of his life. It was less hassle, and no one was pushing him to have children. The only person he had to rely on was himself.

Then Cecily had turned up, and she had left him wondering what it would be like to be married. She had been timid and sweet, but hardworking and devoted to her husband. Lewis could see her being perfect for him, but she was already married, and he wasn't about to break that up; he respected the sanctity of marriage, and he wouldn't break up a happy couple for his own selfish needs.

He had been devastated when his friend and neighbor died, and Cecily was left alone. But he made a promise to himself that he wouldn't desert her; Cecily needed all the support he could give. Lewis didn't mind being that support. Then he spent more time with her, and he began to realize maybe he had done the wrong thing. Instead of keeping himself distant, he was falling more and more in love with her. It was not a good thing.

He should have walked away, but now Cecily had given birth, and she was, essentially, on her own with Oliver, Lewis knew he couldn't walk away, not now. What had surprised him was that Oliver was a delight. That would probably change as he started getting more mobile and started to talk, but Lewis found he liked the baby stage. It was hard work, but also adorable.

If you had children of your own, you would be able to have this every day.

Only if Cecily was their mother.

He was a fool for falling in love with someone who wasn't available. She wasn't really available now, and yet Lewis still found himself hoping. That needed to stop.

But he knew it wouldn't. He just couldn't stop.

"Lewis."

Lewis turned. Christian was coming around the side of the house. He was wiping his face down with a cloth and tugging down his shirt sleeves.

"Has Mrs. Tamberi gone?"

"She has, although she's threatening to come back tomorrow to talk some sense into her daughter." Christian shook his head. "I've seen stubborn people in my time, but Mrs. Tamberi is right up there with the worst of them."

"I have to agree with you on that." Lewis adjusted his hold on Oliver as the baby squealed and flapped his arms towards Christian with a giggle. "I think someone wants to say hello."

Christian smiled and reached out to touch Oliver's hand.

"Hey, little man. You're getting bigger, aren't you?"

"Do you want to hold him a moment? My arms are getting tired."

"Wimp. I have to carry heavier than this little lad regularly with my children."

"You're bigger and stronger than I am. You can manage it without any problems."

"You're still a wimp." Christian chuckled as he eased Oliver out of Lewis' arms. "Come on, let's get you inside. It's starting to get chilly."

Lewis hadn't really noticed. The heat coming from the baby had actually kept him warm, much to his surprise. He followed Christian into the house, and they went into the living room where the fire was barely dwindling. Christian settled down on the settee with the child on his knee.

"Why don't you stoke up the fire and I'll entertain this little one?"

"Why me?"

"Because you left me to do the work at the printers, and I had to physically carry Mrs. Tamberi away. I think I deserve a little bit of a reward."

Lewis rolled his eyes and began to build up the fire again, glancing over at the occasional giggle to see Christian bouncing Oliver on his knee before making Oliver lean back so he could tickle his tummy. Oliver seemed to be enjoying himself, and Christian was looking more relaxed than he had been earlier. Despite knowing that Christian had a wife and several children waiting for him at home and that his playing with Oliver was purely innocent, Lewis felt a twinge of jealousy. His older brother was so easy-going with babies. It just came so easily to him.

For some reason, he didn't want that. He wanted that easy-going nature to be just for him and Oliver and nobody else.

"Where's Cecily?" Christian adjusted Oliver on his lap and looked up. "Is she all right?"

"She fell asleep a short while ago. I think she's just exhausted after facing her mother."

"I feel drained after dealing with her. I'm not surprised she is."

Lewis finished bringing the fire back up to its former state, and then he collapsed onto the settee beside his brother.

"I just wish I knew what to do. It's not fair that Cecily has to do all this without her husband. Having her mother spreading lies and being rude towards her is just ridiculous."

"Some parents behave differently, but Felicity Tamberi is one of those people who just plows straight through without caring what anyone else thinks." Christian frowned. "How Cecily is her daughter, I have no idea. Or how she's related to that family. They are all spoiled brats."

"They weren't always like that. I seem to remember they were decent people when we were younger."

"I know, but the moment that woman married Jackson Tamberi, things changed. She's just... overbearing."

"More than overbearing." Lewis went on. "I think it's safe to say she just marches in and takes over whenever she can. It seems to be something she's really good at."

Christian grunted.

"Cecily's been holding out against her for a while now. But without her husband around, I can see her cracking soon."

"So can I." Lewis shuddered. "And when that happens, she's back in the family. She may not want it, but it's going to happen."

"You don't want that to happen."

It wasn't a question. And Lewis wasn't going to deny it. He shook his head. "Absolutely not. I want her to stay here. With me, if possible."

"Then why don't you tell her? The least you could do is tell her that you've been in love with her for months."

"She might see it as an obligation. I don't want to do that to her."

"How is it an obligation. Just tell her the truth." Christian bounced Oliver on his knee. "It's the least you could do. She deserves to know."

Lewis knew he should. It was going to drive him mad if he saw her walk away and he didn't say anything, but he didn't think he could cope with her saying no. She still loved her husband, didn't she? Lewis couldn't compete with that.

Maybe you can. Maybe you can give her something that she's looking for.

But what?

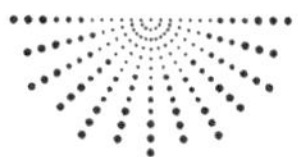

CHAPTER ELEVEN

"Do you think we should wake her up now?" Christian asked. "I've got to head back home, and you have to finish up with the shop."

"Leave her for now. I'll take Oliver with me." Lewis reached over and eased the baby out of his brother's arms. "She is allowed to have a break."

"If I didn't know better, I'd say you were a doting father." Christian chuckled. "I didn't think I would ever be saying that about you."

Lewis didn't think he would be hearing it, either. If it had been a year ago, he would have scoffed at being so close to a baby. And yet, with Oliver in his arms, it felt like the most natural thing in the world.

Why would he want to give that up now?

"Lewis?"

Lewis looked up. Cecily was in the doorway to his workshop, trying to smooth down her hair. There was a crease mark on her cheek from where she had been sleeping. That just made her look even more adorable.

"I take it you needed that sleep."

"I suppose I did. I wasn't expecting that." Cecily winced as she looked at her son, sleeping soundly in the sling Lewis had made across his chest. "I do feel awful, though. I'm supposed to be a mother and be there for my son, and yet I can't be awake for him."

"Don't worry about it. Christian and I are more than happy to help out."

Cecily sighed and lowered her head.

"Maybe Mother is right. Maybe I am a neglectful mother, maybe I need her help."

Lewis didn't want to hear that. He came around the printing press and approached her, taking Cecily's hand and giving it a little shake.

"Don't think like that. She has no idea what she's saying. You're a great mother and you are allowed to have a break every now and then. With the stress she's putting you under I'm amazed that you're still standing."

"I didn't mean to have a sleep." Cecily protested. "But after arguing with Mother, I just…"

"Had all your energy sucked out of you."

Cecily nodded, her head still down. Lewis didn't want to see her like this. He looked down at Oliver in the sling, hearing him snore softly. He had been quite happy to cuddle up to Lewis as he worked, and he had been sleeping like an angel for the last half-hour.

"Why don't you take him now? I'm sure he's going to wake up soon to be fed. I've got an errand to run."

"At this time of night?" Cecily looked up. "Where are you going?"

"I'll tell you later. Can you help me with the sling?"

Cecily did, easing her son out of the sling so Lewis could undo the strip of cloth and put it to one side. Then he rolled down the sleeves of his shirt and unhooked his jacket from a nearby hook.

"I'll come by later to see you… if that's all right? I want to know if you are feeling better."

"There's no need to do that." Cecily shook her head. "You've done a lot for me already."

"And I'll keep on doing it." Lewis brushed his fingers across her cheek, giving her a smile. "It'll put my mind at rest."

Cecily looked like she was going to argue. Finally, she sighed and nodded.

"All right. If it will make you feel better."

"Thank you." Lewis hesitated. Then he kissed her cheek. "I'll see you later."

He hurried out of the workshop before Cecily could respond, striding off down the street. He was aware that he had left the workshop unlocked, but right now Lewis didn't really care. He had other things to think about for now. However, Cecily didn't need to know what it was, right now.

Not until he had made a fool of himself.

This had better have a point to it. And it had better be fruitful.

I hope it is. I'm sure it will be.

It didn't take long for Lewis to navigate the streets to the slightly richer part of Lubbock and up the hill. The Tamberi family had a very grand-looking house at the top of the hill, overlooking most of the town. Looking up at it, Lewis had problems linking this place with Cecily's childhood. It didn't look like a place she would grow up in at all.

It was certainly a place where a rich woman like Felicity Tamberi would live.

Lewis was sweating as he headed up to the front door and rang the bell. He could feel the sweat trickling down his back, but he ignored it. There was something more important than being soaked in sweat. If they didn't like it, then it was tough.

A man wearing a smart black suit that looked like it had been starched within an inch of its life opened the door. He looked Lewis up and down.

"Can I help you, sir?"

"I want to see Mrs. Tamberi."

"The tradesman's entrance is around the side of the house."

Lewis huffed. "I'm not a tradesman. I want to speak to Mrs. Tamberi."

"Mrs. Tamberi is not expecting guests."

"She'll see me."

"Who is it, Charleston?"

Lewis saw Felicity enter the hall from a door off to the side, she was looking very elegant in a dark blue dress with her hair piled up delicately on her head. She did look spectacular, Lewis had to admit that. She stopped when she saw Lewis, and her eyes narrowed.

"What are you doing here?"

"I want to talk to you, Mrs. Tamberi. It's about Cecily."

"I have nothing to say to you, now get out of my sight."

Lewis felt as if he had failed, so much for his big ideas.

CHAPTER TWELVE

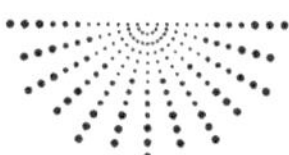

For a moment, Lewis turned to walk away. He had tried and failed but then he thought of Cecily and how she would never get out from under this woman's shadow and it gave him courage.

"How about I just talk to you?" Lewis spread his hands. "We can talk in private, or I can speak to you from here. I don't mind. I'm just going to have my say."

For a moment, he thought Felicity was going to turn down the offer. Then she sighed heavily and waved a hand.

"Let him come in, Charleston. We'll talk in the drawing room."

"Yes, Mrs. Tamberi."

Charleston stepped aside and Lewis entered the house. He tried not to look around with an open mouth as he followed Felicity through the mass of corridors. This place was far too big. Apparently, three generations lived under the same roof and there looked room for more. Lewis was glad he had something small and simple; it was far less hassle to keep clean than this monstrosity.

Felicity led him into a room near the back of the house, her skirts swishing as she went to the window.

"What do you want, Mr. Hancock? Isn't what you said earlier enough or did you need to come back for more?"

"I wanted to tell you to leave Cecily and Oliver alone."

Felicity spun around and stared at him. "You're telling me to keep away from my own daughter and grandson?"

"Yes."

She threw her head back and laughed. "You must be mad. They're part of the family, and Cecily is going to realize that she can't cope without us. She is going to be coming back soon, I'm sure of it."

"Is that why you've been telling lies about her? To force her to come back and beg for forgiveness simply because she chose to marry for love?"

"We had someone lined up for her, and he would have been a better choice. Then, somehow, she found someone who she thought could give her something more." Felicity snorted rudely. "Evidently not, because he's now dead."

Lewis growled. "Her husband was a good man. He would have given her the happiness she deserved and not treated her like she was something unpleasant on his shoe."

"You have no idea how my family behaves. Not that it's any of your business."

"I think I know enough to know that you and your husband, along with your in-laws, are at the top and in charge. Especially you. Then it's your sons, and then it's Cecily. Maybe a servant or two slipped in there before her. In your mind, girls are not worth anything except how well they can marry." Lewis folded his arms. "There's a hierarchy here that is outdated and pathetic. It's no wonder Cecily found someone else to marry and have a life with."

Felicity's nostrils flared. "Did you just call our family pathetic?"

"I called the hierarchy pathetic, but you think whatever you want." Lewis glared at her. "Why are you so determined to make sure Cecily doesn't have a good life? Why do you want her back here and miserable? Shouldn't you want the best for her?"

Felicity sniffed. "As I said, it's none of your business. You wouldn't understand, anyway."

"You're right. I don't understand. Because I like to think I'm a normal person." Lewis took a deep breath. "Look, I'm not here to judge you on what you do or don't do, but I did come to say that you and your family need to stop the lies about Cecily. She's a good mother, and Oliver is very well looked after. She has the necessary support to raise him, and that's not going to change. Your lies are just going to be pointless in the long run. The more you spread them the more determined she will be to stay away. So stop it now."

Felicity's jaw tightened. Pink spots appeared on her cheeks. "Did you just tell me what to do?"

"Yes, I believe I did."

"You're not a parent, Mr. Hancock, so you have no idea how to parent someone, nor do you know what's best."

"I know what's best for Cecily more than you."

Felicity tilted her head to one side. "Why are you here defending her, anyway? Are you in love with her or something?"

Lewis hesitated. He hadn't wanted to say anything to Cecily's mother until he had told Cecily, but he wouldn't back away from it.

"I do love her, Mrs. Tamberi. And I love your grandson. He's an adorable baby, and I hope I can be in his life as more than just a neighbor."

Felicity stared at him. Then she burst out laughing.

"You and my daughter? You must be mad if you think my husband or I are going to agree to that? What rubbish!"

"Who said I was coming here for permission?"

"We get the final say in her life."

Lewis couldn't believe the entitlement of the woman. She just didn't understand.

"I'm not here for permission to court your daughter, or even to marry her. I'm just here to tell you that I won't tolerate you abusing her anymore. She's been through enough, and she deserves some peace and happiness. Just because you're jealous of how well she's done without your help doesn't mean you get to behave in such a manner."

Felicity's face darkened even more.

"Who said I was jealous?"

"Anyone looking at the two of you can tell. You don't like the fact that she's managed to find someone who loves her and has a life outside of your family. You don't control her life, and you don't like it." Lewis shook his head. "Cecily doesn't need to answer to you, and you should leave her alone. If you can't be in her life without taking charge and having things your own way, you shouldn't be in her life at all."

Felicity's mouth opened and closed. She looked like a gaping fish.

"You... what did you say?"

"You heard me, Mrs. Tamberi. I know you're not deaf."

"And I was hoping I hadn't heard you correctly. You just told me to walk out of my daughter's life."

"If you're going to treat her as a possession and not as your daughter, then absolutely, you should leave."

Felicity looked like she was going to pitch a fit. She bared her teeth.

"You have the nerve to come into my house and tell me I shouldn't be anywhere near my grandson. I won't tolerate that. The sheriff will hear about you threatening me."

"Try it. I'm sure he'll be delighted to take it on." Lewis turned away. "I had come here hoping for a heart-to-heart and that maybe we could be adults about this, but that's not going to happen. I'm going to give you the choice of apologizing to Cecily about your actions and start afresh, or you can leave her alone and consider her not a part of the family anymore."

"I'm not going to take orders from you." Felicity hissed.

"Those are your choices, and I hope you do choose wisely. I know Cecily wants you in her life in a more loving capacity, but if you can't bring yourself to do that, then you've lost a child."

"That's up to Cecily, don't you think?"

"I know. But I'm just passing on that I'm on her side, and that she's got me for support." Lewis opened the door and flashed Felicity a smile. "I'm sure you understand. I'll expect your answer tomorrow. If you don't want to make amends and admit you were wrong, then don't bother coming over. I don't want Cecily to get her hopes up. She deserves to have the people who cause her trouble out of her life, including her parents. Good day, Mrs. Tamberi."

Lewis left the room. He was almost back at the front door when he heard someone shrieking and shouting. There was another voice with it, this one deeper and quieter, but it was there. It sounded like the husband had come along to find out what was going on.

Lewis glanced at Charleston as he left the house.

"I have a feeling Mrs. Tamberi is going to need a very large brandy."

He certainly needed one himself after that.

CHAPTER THIRTEEN

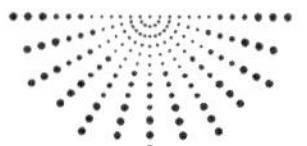

Cecily sat on the edge of her bed and watched as Oliver slept. He had barely stirred when she took him back to the house, choosing to snuggle up against her until he was back in his crib. She felt awful for sleeping most of the day and having other people look after her son. That wasn't the type of person she was at all. But whenever she spoke to her mother, it always turned into an argument. And then she ended up feeling emotionally drained. It had been like that her whole life.

Felicity wanted things done a certain way. Her family had the same archaic opinions, and now Felicity had finally found someone who wanted to marry her, she was determined to become the matriarch and rule with an iron thumb. And nobody called her up on it except for Cecily; they all got something out of it. Felicity favored her husbands and sons and tolerated her in-laws. Cecily was a girl, so she was seen as less important. And yet, all Cecily wanted was to have a mother who loved her.

She vowed that she would never do this to her children. Oliver deserved better, he would get to make his own choices.

If only they could sit down and talk rationally about it. Cecily wanted her parents in her life, but if they were going to be rude about her choices and call her a bad mother, there wasn't really much point. That hurt to think about, but it was for the best. She could make sure they didn't make Oliver feel awful whenever he was around his maternal relatives.

As long as he grew up feeling loved. That's what she wanted for him.

A sound out in the street had Cecily looking up. Then she heard the loud creak that came from Lewis's work-shop door. She sat up. Was he back? Or was someone breaking in?

. . .

Leaving Oliver in his crib, Cecily hurried downstairs and to the front door. She opened it and collided with a tall, hard body that made her practically bounce off. Hands grabbed her and held her up as her feet buckled.

"Careful there! Where's the fire?"

It was Lewis. Cecily sagged in relief.

"Lewis! I thought someone was breaking into your workshop!"

"That was only me. I was locking up properly." Lewis waited until Cecily got her footing back. "Are you all right?"

"I am now." She peered up at him. "What happened? Where did you go?"

Lewis didn't answer for a moment. Then he drew her into his arms. "I'll tell you in a moment."

"What..."

Cecily started as Lewis kissed her. For a split second, her mind was spinning. Was this actually happening? Was Lewis actually kissing her? Then her body melted and she sank into his arms. He was far sweeter with his kiss than she expected. This was not what she thought would happen at all.

Lewis kept the kiss light, pulling away slowly.

Cecily heard a whimper and realized it was coming from her. Opening her eyes, she stared at him.

"What was that for?"

"It's something I've wanted to do for a very long time." Lewis swallowed. "You don't mind, do you?"

"You're asking me that after you've just kissed me."

"I know, but..."

Cecily grabbed his head and pulled him down so that she could kiss him again. Lewis stiffened for a moment, but then he returned the kiss, his arms tightening around her. Cecily eased back, her lips throbbing. It had been a long time since she had kissed anyone, and it felt nice as well as strange. Mostly nice.

"I will mind if you stop kissing me. And I will mind if you don't tell me what you've been doing."

Lewis sighed. "I suppose I do owe you an explanation. I went to see your mother."

"My mother?" Cecily stared at him. "Why would you do that?"

"Because I wanted to tell her that she was pushing you further away with her actions and that she had an opportunity to actually make amends and respect your choices. That you weren't to be bullied anymore."

Cecily was trying to get her head around Lewis going to her former family home to confront her mother.

"But... why? What did you hope to gain from doing that?"

"I wanted her to stop. I wanted you and Oliver to be left alone." Lewis looked sheepish. "If she's a smart woman, she'll understand my point of view. But if she chooses to stay on her high horse and refuses to apologize, you'll know then how much she values you."

Cecily didn't think her mother had gotten off her high horse in years. She stepped back from Lewis.

"But why would you do that? I didn't ask you to."

"You didn't need to. I did it because I wanted you to be safe, and you'll always be on edge with your mother harassing you and calling you those horrid names."

Lewis spread his hands. "That's not how I want the future to be for you."

"I can take care of her."

"You don't want someone in your corner?"

"Of course, but..." Cecily swallowed. "That's too much to ask of you. I couldn't ask you to fight on my behalf."

"You want to do it alone?"

"I'd rather not do it at all."

Lewis's expression softened.

"I'll always be in your corner, Cecily. I have been since you moved in."

"What are you...?" Cecily frowned. "What are you saying, Lewis? I don't think I understand."

"Then understand this." Lewis took her hands and kissed her knuckles, never taking his eyes off her. "I swore myself off marriage and children years ago. I told myself I didn't need it in my life. But then you came along, and I realized that I did need it."

The words were going around Cecily's head, but they weren't really sinking in.

"What... what do you mean?"

"I mean you made me believe I could have a future and a family for myself. You could make me change my mind. The fact you were married was a problem, and I would never come between you and your husband. But since..." Lewis cleared his throat. "Since his death, and you having Oliver, the ache to tell you how I felt has been building, and it's getting too much. I hate seeing how upset you were getting regarding your family, and I wanted to do something to help."

Was he saying that he loved her? Cecily felt like she was solving a riddle. She frowned.

"Are you saying what I think you're saying?" she asked. "Did you just say you...?"

"That I love you? That for the first time in my life I can see myself settling down and having a family because of you? Yes, I am."

He sounded so certain of himself, so calm. Cecily felt like the world wasn't quite real.

"Is that why you let me work for you? Because you loved me?"

"Because I wanted to help. I wasn't about to charge in and declare my love while your husband was barely cold in his grave, was I?" Lewis rubbed the back of his neck. "I would have said nothing for far longer, but I'm a fool. By the time I gathered my courage, you would have moved on or gone back to your family. I didn't want that."

"I don't ever want to go back to my family."

"I didn't know that, and I didn't want to take that chance." Lewis' expression flickered. Now he looked uncertain. "So, Cecily, how about it? About us? Could you see yourself loving me eventually?"

What a ridiculous question. Cecily laughed. Lewis looked hurt.

"There's nothing funny about that. I'm opening myself up here," he said.

"I'm only laughing at how daft the question is." Cecily cupped his face in her hands. "I love you already. So seeing myself loving you is actually quite easy."

Now it was Lewis' turn to look dazed.

"You mean it?"

"I do." Cecily kissed him. "And I'm very prepared to say that several times over if you get my meaning."

"I have a feeling that you just proposed to me."

"Well, I'm the one with the most experience of weddings."

Lewis groaned, wrapping his arms around her. "I'm going to have my work cut out with you as my wife, aren't I?"

"Mother and I are alike in that we're tenacious. But I do know where to draw the line." Cecily brushed her lips over his. "And when I'm very sure of what's in front of me, I go out and get it. Including a man who's willing to stand up to my family for me."

"I'll stand up to anyone for you." Lewis kissed her forehead. "Just as long as I get to come home and know you and Oliver are there waiting for me. That will make me happy."

Cecily had no doubt about it. It certainly made her happy knowing that her neighbor and the man she had fallen for was prepared to do anything for her. Even scolding her mother. She would have loved to have seen that.

Maybe one day. Right now, she was content with what she had.

"Do you want to come in for a bit?" Cecily asked. "I'm more awake now, and I'm hungry. I can make dinner."

Lewis smiled. "I'd like nothing better."

EPILOGUE

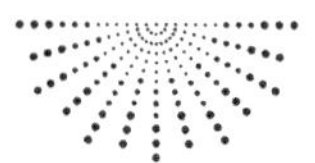

Jake leaned against the wall and listened to the festivities inside. He could hear the laughter and the music; Cecily had been insistent on lots of dancing at her wedding. Lewis had just gone along with it.

Jake had known Lewis for thirty years since they were barely walking. He had witnessed Lewis grow up, knew his preferences about marriage and children, and thought his friend would be dying a bachelor with him being the last of his line. Lewis had been adamant about that. Now he was married with a stepson. Jake was beginning to wonder if the same man who had just gotten married was the same man he grew up with.

But he couldn't begrudge Lewis for changing his mind. It had to take one particular person to make him think differently, and Cecily had come along. True, their circumstances weren't ideal in the beginning, but Lewis had been a gentleman about it. He never overstepped his mark, and he was respectful of Cecily's boundaries. Jake had thought Lewis would never say anything.

Evidently, that had changed.

Lewis deserved it. He needed true happiness in his life. And Cecily deserved to be happy as well. She had been practically glowing as Lewis said his vows to her, and Jake didn't think she had stopped smiling. After losing her husband and going through a dark time, she finally had something to help her settle down. Jake knew Lewis would be able to do that; he was a solid, dependable man.

It was a shame that her family didn't think so. Jake had no idea what Lewis had said to Felicity Tamberi, but it had left her storming away and vowing that Cecily was not a part of their family anymore. Since then, they had kept their distance. As far as Jake was aware, she had never gotten a chance to meet Oliver properly, and now she was saying she didn't want to meet him.

It was sad that a grandmother would throw her daughter and grandson away, but it didn't seem to bother Cecily. She seemed lighter, happier. Calmer. It was startling how things could make people change. Knowing that her family wasn't breathing down her neck and trying to bring her back into the fold seemed to have lifted a weight off her shoulders.

At least the complaints that Oliver was being neglected had stopped. Jake was glad about that; he could easily tell that Oliver wasn't being hurt or neglected. Anyone who looked at the boy knew that. But Felicity hadn't been about to stop. It was just ridiculous and petty. At least now, he didn't have to go over and tell Cecily about the new complaint; it was a waste of time.

Jake would be happy if he didn't have to deal with that woman Cecily had to call a mother ever again. The family was always going to be there, and their name was impossible to ignore, but as long as they left Cecily and Lewis alone, things would co-exist quite nicely.

The music momentarily stopped, and Jake contemplated going back inside. He didn't mind the occasional festivities, but for some reason, everyone seemed to want to come to a wedding. Even Emma; the former midwife was getting obsessed. She loved going to weddings and seeing a couple she had played a part in putting together show their love for one another.

As far as he knew, Emma hadn't played a part in Cecily and Lewis getting together. But Jake wouldn't be surprised if she was involved.

Maybe he should head back home and just have a bit of time in the quiet. It would stop his head pounding, and it would also stop him from thinking about what could have happened if he had actually managed to get married to the woman he loved. However, that wasn't going to happen, not when Jake was such a coward.

He didn't deserve love when he couldn't tell the one person he could see being married to that he loved her. He had had a chance, and now he had missed it. There was no second chance, not with everything going on in her life right now. Jake couldn't see her wanting to get married again.

Pushing off the wall, Jake adjusted his Stetson and shoved his hands into his pockets. He would head home and have an early night. Lewis would understand, and he had celebrated with him for most of the wedding. Nobody would notice if the sheriff disappeared.

He set off home. At least his home wasn't too far away, and the night was drawing in and becoming rather chilly. Jake could feel it ruffling his collar and a chill going down his back. That was horrible. He didn't like the cold. It was bad enough with snow that they got in town every now and then without the biting wind. Jake shivered and hurried on.

As he got closer to his house, Jake slowed. He could see someone at the door, hovering there just out of the shadows. As far as he was aware, he wasn't expecting anyone, and anyone who needed him for a crime would go to his workplace. Nobody bothered him at home.

He moved closer and saw it was a tall, raven-haired woman wearing a dark green coat over a pale green dress. Her hair was loose about her shoulders and trailed down her back, almost to her waist. Her arms were wrapped around her middle, and she seemed to be shivering.

Jake felt a prickling on the back of his neck. Even from behind, he recognized his visitor.

Opening the gate, he headed up the path.

"Georgina?"

Georgina Hunt turned. She was looking paler than he remembered, and she did look a little thinner. But there was a sharpness in her eyes that hadn't been there the last time he saw her. It looked like she was back in control of herself. She gave him a small smile.

"Hey, Jake."

For a moment, Jake didn't know what to say. He knew what he wanted to do, but grabbing someone to kiss them was going to have him getting slapped. He swallowed.

"When did you get back?"

"A couple of hours ago. I thought it..." Georgina bit her lip. "Well, I'm better. I like to think I am, and I needed to come back to start afresh."

She was better. Jake didn't know if he believed that. The last time he had seen her, he had sent Georgina to her family's home in Phoenix after she tried to take a baby by force and was carrying a knife, intent on doing harm. Thankfully, nobody had been hurt, and everyone had been understanding that her mind had been stretched to the point where things were misconstrued and she was hallucinating. But Jake didn't know if he could believe she was better, until he saw it.

Even then, he still wanted to hold onto her and not let go.

"I see."

"I know you think I'm telling you whatever, but believe me, I am feeling better. I'm not as... chaotic as I was before, and I don't have an urge to go out and kidnap babies." Georgina flinched. "That makes me sound really awful, doesn't it?"

"You were having a breakdown. It's a normal thing to happen."

"I'm sure Ben Andrews has something else to say about that." Georgina tucked her hair behind her ear. "That's why I need to talk to you. I'm sorry it's late, but I need your help. Can you help me? I know I haven't given you a reason to, but I don't know who else to talk to."

Jake had known that his one and only weakness would be Georgina. Ever since they met, he knew she would have him doing something stupid if she even asked. In spite of what happened, that hadn't changed. And Jake really wanted to help. He headed towards the door.

"Come on in. Then you can talk to me about what you need help with."

Hopefully, he wouldn't regret this.

If you missed any of the books in this amazing series you can find them all here

Read on for a preview of the next book...

Georgina could feel her heart racing as Jake drove the wagon up to the ranch. She had asked to do this, but now she was beginning to doubt herself. Nerves were beginning to set in, and she had an urge to jump off the wagon and run back to town.

What if Ben didn't forgive her? What if he and Madeleine threw her out? Georgina wouldn't blame them if they did that, but she hoped that they would listen to her, at least.

Even as she tried to talk herself into staying, her mouth was dry, she was getting a headache and her palms were hot and sweaty. She rubbed her hands on her skirts, wishing she didn't feel like she was going to faint.

Her family kept saying that she was a failure, that she wouldn't amount to anything. Now she had shown that they were right. She was told over and over again that she was destined to be labeled as crazy, and nobody was going to listen to her.

Georgina wanted to prove them wrong. She was not insane. She had been going through grief, and it had manifested in the wrong way. That was all. But her family, especially her parents, declared that she was a danger to everyone.

Her mental state was going to get worse if she stayed with them. Georgina needed to get out and prove them wrong, but could she?

Jake pulled the wagon up outside the ranch house and jumped out. He turned and hesitated when he looked at her. The dark-haired beauty's normal olive skin was pale. She was trying so hard and he wished he could ease her distress. However, this was one thing she had to face.

"Georgina?"

Georgina didn't answer. She couldn't even look at him. Jake was putting himself out bringing her here, and she felt awful, wanting to tell him to go back as she was losing her nerve.

Jake hauled himself back up, sitting across from her.

"You can do this, Georgina. This is a big step, but you're here now. You can do it."

"I'm scared, Jake. I want to run away." Georgina could feel herself shaking. She was going to start crying at any moment, she just knew it. "I don't think I can face them."

Jake's expression softened. He took her hands. "You can face them. I'll be with you all the time. We'll talk to Ben and Madeleine, and we'll do it slowly. Start to finish, as we agreed."

"But what if they don't want to hear me? What if they throw me out?"

"I sent a message ahead that you wanted to talk to them. I haven't had anything back, so I see that as a good sign. Ben and Madeleine are rational people, they will listen."

"I wanted to kidnap Ben's child and I threatened Madeleine with a knife! How are they going to get past that?"

"You don't know until you try. They understand you were under a lot of stress, and it's been a few months now."

Georgina knew that. She had been painfully aware of all the days after she made a mistake and tried to take a child that wasn't hers by force. But things had been twisted in her head, and she was grasping onto something she believed would make her happy. It had backfired on her, and Georgina knew she was lucky that she hadn't been arrested.

"Take a few deep breaths, Georgina." Jake gave her a gentle smile. "The fact you're here says a lot. I'll be right beside you, and I won't leave you alone."

"Promise?"

"I promise."

That did make her feel a little better. Jake had promised that he would look after her, and he was keeping hold of his promise. He had been like that before Georgina got married, something she remembered and appreciated. The sheriff had never backed away whenever she needed help.

He did when you went back to your family.

My family promised to look after me. And they failed. That's not his fault.

"Georgina?"

"I..." Georgina licked her lips. "Just don't leave me alone. And I want to stay outside. It will make it easier to leave if they want me to."

"Of course." Jake squeezed her fingers and started to climb down, pausing as he put a foot on the ground. "Here they come."

Georgina looked up, her heart almost stopping when she saw Ben and Madeleine Andrews coming out onto the porch. Both of them were wearing grim expressions, and Ben was wearing a gun holster. Georgina noted that his hand was settled on his belt, very near to the gun handle.

While she could understand, that didn't help her fight back her panic.

"Come on." Jake jumped down and turned to her. "You've got this."

"Can I just stay here and talk to them?"

"No. You know you can do this, Georgina." He held out a hand. "I won't let go of you."

Grab Love for the Sheriff here

MAIL ORDER BRIDES
TEXAS MAIL ORDER BRIDES
LOVE FOR THE
SHERIFF
INDIANA WAKE
& BELLE FIFFER

ALSO BY INDIANA WAKE

Find out about new releases, get special offers, and receive 3
free books by joining my exclusive newsletter
http://eepurl.com/gP7I6n

A Bride to Save the Rancher

If you would like to find all of my books, look on my Amazon page

While there, click the yellow follow button for updates.

God bless,

Indiana Wake

Indiana Wake was born in Denver, Colorado, where she learned to love the outdoors and horses. At the age of eleven, her parents moved to the United Kingdom to follow her father's career.

It was a strange and foreign new world, and it took a while for her to settle down. Her mom raised horses and Indiana soon learned to ride. She would often escape on horseback imagining she was back in the Wild West. As well as horses, Indiana escaped into fiction and dreamed of all the friends she had left behind.

From an early age, she loved stories. They were always sweet and clean and, more often than not, included horses, cowboys and most importantly of all a happy ever after. As she got older, she would often be found making up her own stories and would tell them to anyone who would listen.

As she grew up, she continued to write, but marriage and a job stole some of her dreams. Then one day she was discussing with a friend at church, how hard it was to get sweet and clean fiction. Though very shy about her writing Indiana agreed to share one of her stories. That friend loved the story and suggested she publish it on kindle. Together they worked really hard, and the rest, as they say, is history.

Indiana has had multiple number one bestsellers and now makes her living from her writing. She believes she was truly blessed to be given this opportunity and thanks each and every one of her readers for making her dream come true.

©Copyright 2022 Indiana Wake
All Rights Reserved

License Notes
This story is a work of fiction any resemblance to people is purely coincidence. All places, names, events, businesses, etc. are used in a fictional manner. All characters are from the imagination of the author.

www.ingramcontent.com/pod-product-compliance
Lightning Source LLC
Chambersburg PA
CBHW052107150726
48002CB00006B/2257